One Alley Summer

MARBLE PRESS

Library of Congress Cataloging-in-Publication
Data has been applied for.

ISBNs: 978-1-958325-12-4 (hardback),
978-1-958325-13-1 (ebook).

Printed in China. First Edition: May 2024.

10 9 8 7 6 5 4 3 2 1

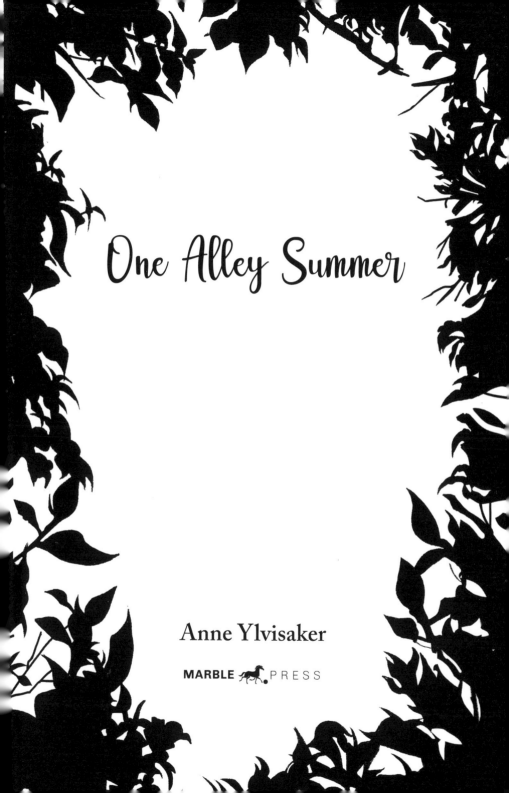

One Alley Summer

Anne Ylvisaker

MARBLE PRESS

To Cara and Nils,
my first best friends.

—A. Y.

I was a Phoebe—nothing more
a Phoebe—nothing less—
The little note that others dropt
I fitted into place—

I dwelt too low that any seek—
too Shy, that any blame—
A Phoebe makes a little print
Upon the Floors of Fame

—Emily Dickinson